Come on!

This way!

ORCHARD BOOKS

First published in Great Britain in 2017 by The Watts Publishing Group

13 5 7 9 10 8 6 4 2

Text © Giles Andreae, 2017
Illustrations © Jess Mikhail, 2017

The moral rights of the author and illustrator have been asserted.

A CIP catalogue record for this book is available from the British Library.

ISBN 978 1 40832 937 5

Printed and bound in China

Orchard Books
An imprint of Hachette Children's Group
Part of The Watts Publishing Group Limited
Carmelite House
50 Victoria Embankment
London EC4Y 0DZ

An Hachette UK Company
www.hachette.co.uk

www.hachettechildrens.co.uk

Quickly!

For the Nit Queen. You know who you are! With love, Giles.

For Lizzy Simpson – J.M.

Hi! Nice to meet you!
What a lovely day!
I'm going to the garden
Would you like to come and play?

But hang on just a minute –

I think I've got an itch.

Yes, I'm pretty sure my head

Needs a good hard scritch!

And just as I scratch it . . .

LOOK OUT! There he goes!

A little naughty nit goes and

jumps up on my nose!

Aaaaghhhh!

Itch

scratch

scritch,

There are nits in my hair!

Those

scritchy

scratchy nits

Are getting everywhere!

There are **nits** in the treetops,

Nits in the playground,
Nits playing chase.

Nits flying rocket ships
And blasting into space!

Nits watching football,

Nits eating sweets.

Nits making pancakes

And stuffing them with treats!

Nits at the **seaside**, nits in the park,
Nits playing **kiss-chase** …

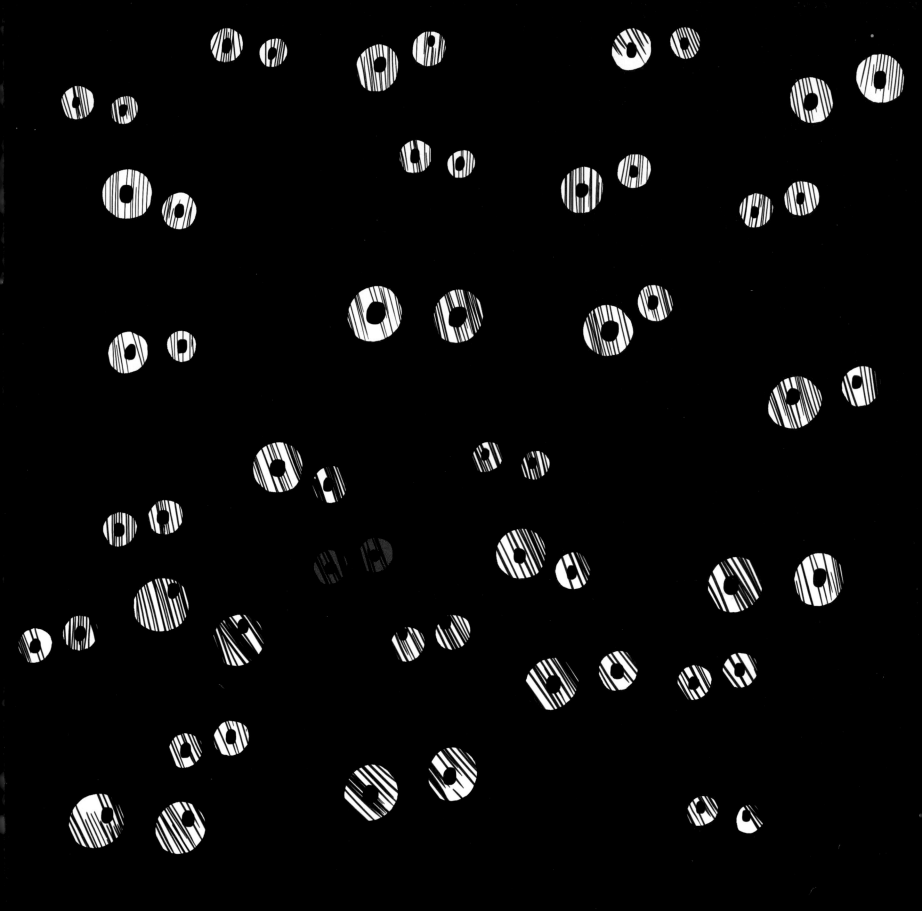

 . . . And **murder-in-the-dark.**

Nits at the disco,

Busting out the moves.

Nits who are rock stars,

Funking to the grooves.

Nits in the bedroom, sleeping safe

and sound.

Nits in the **nuddy**

When there's no one else around.

But here comes

my mummy

NIT ZAP

With her **shampoo**
and her **comb**.

Those **nits** will

neVer

beat her.

No, those **nits** are

going home!

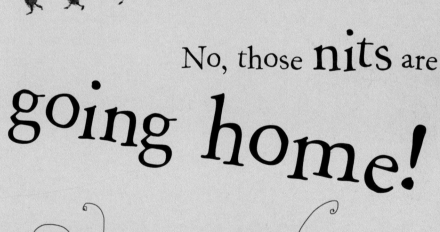

And now my head is free of **nits**.

They've scoot-skidaddled!

GONE!

But they're looking for **another** head . . .